THE CHAMPION

MICHAEL KINGSWOOD

CONTENTS

THE CHAMPION

When I was little I had a recurring dream where I became weightless and floated up from my bed. I would always cringe as the ceiling approached, expecting a painful impact. But instead, I simply penetrated the ceiling, then the roof above, and floated up into the night sky. I wafted on the breeze, rising higher until I passed the top of the great elm tree in our front yard.

I always felt a giddy sensation as the whole neighborhood spread out beneath me like the maps in the atlas I kept in my room. All those houses, so large and sprawling on the ground, became tiny as the models in an electric train set, making me giggle with glee.

As I floated higher, the breeze became a blowing wind that carried me swiftly away to the south. My house vanished before long, leaving me with a vague feeling of unease. But that feeling was quickly swept away by the sheer exhilaration of flight.

I zoomed through the air, rising higher and faster toward the heavens. The stars grew brighter as I left the lights of human settlements behind, filling my gaze with billions of pinpoints of light. Somewhere in the back of my mind I knew I should be getting cold as I got higher – wasn't that why tall mountains had snow on them? – but instead all I felt was a pleasant, soothing warmth flowing through my limbs, despite the fact that I was wearing only light pajamas.

Higher still I ascended and a single star, blue-white and brighter than the others, grabbed my attention. Brighter and brighter it grew, and it almost seemed to be moving toward me. Or maybe it was just that I was by then moving so quickly that it just looked that way. Regardless, the star soon filled my vision completely, and I wondered why I could still see clearly.

Then, with a great flash of blue light, the night sky disappeared and I found myself in a small, pleasant room. A fireplace crackled in the corner, lending light, heat, and the cheerful odor of wood smoke to the room. Opposite the fireplace was a small window with drapes that were decorated with airplanes and rocket ships. The window looked out onto a grassy field with a brilliant collection of stars overhead. There was a narrow door on one wall, the room's only exit besides the window.

A pair of rocking chairs with quilted cushions stood facing the fireplace, a small end table between them. Two mugs of hot steaming liquid sat on the table. The chair on the left was occupied. An old man, wispy gray hair hanging over his brows and a broad grey mustache above his lips, rocked slowly in the chair, making a soft creaking noise each time the chair leaned backward. He was dressed in an old fashioned brown tweed jacket, the kind with pads on the elbows, and matching pants. His shirt was off-white, and buttoned all the way up to the collar, where he wore a brown and yellow bow tie.

It would always take him a minute or so to notice me. When he did, he smiled the warm and welcoming smile of a man who has seen a dear old friend and gestured for me to join him in the other rocking chair. I did, and helped myself to one of the steaming cups without waiting to be asked. It was set out there for me, after all. Hot chocolate with marshmallows, my favorite.

We rocked in silence for a time, just watching the fire slowly consume the logs in the fireplace and sipping on the hot chocolate. It was so pleasant that I found myself thinking how easy it would be to just fall asleep there. How soothing it would be.

Then I would remind myself I was already asleep and this was just a dream.

And always then the old man would laugh and turn to look me in the eye. "Of course it's a dream, Timothy," he said, and winked. "But if you're going to dream, it might as well have hot chocolate in it, hmm?"

I giggled in response and he leaned over in his chair. When he came back up, he had a picture book in his hands.

"Would you like to hear a story?"

I nodded and he opened the book. It was always a different story, but with a theme I recognized and loved. The evil king captured the helpless princess. Or was it a prince, or a mystical artifact, or a book of learning? It was always different, but always a brave knight rode to the rescue, defeating the evil king and saving the day.

The stories always left me feeling excited but also confused. Who was the evil king and why could the knight never defeat him? He always rode to the rescue, but the king always returned to do more dastardly deeds.

When I asked, the old man simply shrugged and sighed a bit sadly. "He has allies," he said, knuckling his mustache softly. "As long as there are people of ill will, the king cannot be beaten forever. He can be driven off, made to lay low for a time, but never truly defeated." He perked up then and, looking back at me, cuffed me on the shoulder playfully.

"Which is why we will always need brave knights to face him. We wouldn't want him to win, would we?"

I chuckled and said no, then finished off the last of my hot chocolate and set the mug down on the table.

The old man nodded and closed the book. "Well you'd best run on home now."

I did not want to go, but I knew he was right so I stood up. That was usually when I woke up in my own bed.

But one time, the old man seemed troubled. He finished the story then sat in silence, his eyes distant as he stared into the flames. After a time, I decided it was time for me to leave so I stood and went to the door. I reached my hand out to the doorknob but flinched away when the old man's voice barked out behind me.

"No!"

I turned around and found him standing up straight, no longer slouching. He was tall, taller than I thought from seeing him in the chair. His lips were drawn back in a scowl, his eyes dark with power.

He frightened me for a moment, but he must have seen it in my face because his scowl faded quickly, replaced by a gentle smile, and his eyes returned to their usual pale blue color. He stepped over to me, placed his hands on my shoulders, and gave them a gentle squeeze.

"You are not ready to go through that door," he said, his voice kind. "Maybe someday. Lord willing, perhaps you will never have to." Then he smiled more broadly, whatever care he had earlier seeming to evaporate. "Go and rest, young knight. Until we meet again."

But we never did. I never dreamed those dreams again after that night.

On occasion I would feel their lack and wonder why the dreams never returned. Of all my childhood dreams, those were the only ones I could remember with any consistency. I cannot recall any others where I knew I was dreaming either. It did not seem right that they should just stop.

But they did, and it did not take very long before the normal rigors of life brought different dreams at night, and during the day as well. I went to school, got a girlfriend, graduated, moved on to college, got a different girlfriend, changed majors three times and girlfriends five times, and finally settled into a career that I enjoyed, designing and building houses for a prominent architecture firm.

Life was good. I was successful at my job and the money flowed well. I was healthy. I got to travel a lot. I had a girl I was serious about. There was nothing to complain about and everything to be happy over.

Until that fateful day, a month before my thirtieth birthday.

❧ 2 ❧

We had just adjourned from a meeting with the firm's biggest client. I had labored day and night for weeks to get the designs to match his exacting requirements. Each meeting before had ended in page after page of changes to make, making me wonder if I would ever see the end of it. But now he had finally signed off on the final design and given the go ahead to begin construction.

Walking back to my office, it was like a weight had been lifted from my shoulders.

I keep a bottle of scotch in the bureau behind my drafting desk for just this sort of occasion. Jim, my immediate superior at the firm, and I had just poured ourselves two fingers each when Helen, my admin, stuck her head in.

"Tim, there's a Mr. Bartleby here to see you," she said. "He says he's an old friend of yours."

I blinked and looked at Helen in confusion. Bartleby? I could not remember ever meeting a Bartleby. I opened my mouth to tell her to make an appointment for later, but Jim beat me to the punch.

"I'll get out of here so you two can catch up," he said, draining his glass in a quick gulp. "Great work, Ace."

I grimaced. Ace was sort of a nickname that senior management at the firm had for me. It made me uncomfortable, but they seemed to enjoy using it so I did not have the heart to ask them to stop.

"Thanks," I managed.

Jim clapped me on the arm and left the office, nodding to Helen as he walked past her.

She rolled her eyes at his back and smirked then looked back at me. "I'll show him in," she said and backed out of the office.

I sighed and took a quick drink, then turned and tucked the glass behind one of the pictures on top of the bureau.

Whoever this Bartleby was, he had cojones to come here claiming to be my friend. He was probably some high roller with delusions of grandeur who did not want to wait to get on my schedule. Regardless, it would not do for a potential client to see me drinking in the office during working hours.

The office door swung open again while my back was turned and Helen said, "Mr. Bartleby, sir."

The door shut and I heard the man take a couple steps toward the chairs I used for receiving clients. I squared my shoulders and turned around.

"Look Mr. Bartleby, I don't know who you..."

The words caught in my throat as I beheld him. He was tall. I'm not a short guy by any measure, but he had me beat by at least two or three inches. He wore a navy blue pinstriped suit that was obviously tailor-made, probably from expensive silk, and a blue and red power tie. But it was his face that stopped me cold. Pale blue eyes below bushy grey brows. A wide grey mustache over a broad mouth that seemed to want to curl up into a smile at any moment. And wispy grey hair that hung to just below his brows.

"Hello, young knight," he said.

His voice was like a key turning in a lock. Memories rushed back, every one of those strange dreams from my childhood surging to the forefront in a rush. My jaw dropped and I stumbled backwards a step.

"Who...?" I began, then stopped and swallowed. "How...?"

The old man chuckled and set his briefcase - I had not even realized he was carrying one - onto my drafting desk. "I realize we were not properly introduced before. Bartleby," he said, "Cornelius Bartleby." He flicked open the latches of his briefcase and opened it. Reaching inside, he withdrew a weathered picture book then looked up at me. "Would you like to hear a story?"

What the hell was this? My mind raced, trying to come to terms with it. It was a joke, that was it.

"Did Jeremy put you up to this? It's not funny." Jeremy was my oldest friend. I had known him since we both were in first grade and he was the only one I had ever told about the dreams. It would be just like him to pull this kind of a prank as a pre-birthday gag.

Bartleby's eyebrows quirked upward. "I know a Jeremy, young knight, but he is eight years old in Nottingham, England."

"Don't call me that!" I snapped. "Who the hell are you?"

Bartleby shook his head slowly and cracked the book open. "Once upon a time there was a..."

I cut him off with a snarl. "Shut up! I don't want to hear your bloody story. You need to leave. Now."

Bartleby sighed and closed the book then looked up at me with earnest eyes. "I'm afraid I can't do that, Timothy. Would you mind having a seat, so I can explain?" He gestured toward the chairs on the far side of my office.

I thought of having Helen call security, but looking Bartleby in the eye gave me pause. There was no malice there, just a sort of kind warmth overlaying a deeper tension, almost like he was deathly afraid of something.

I swallowed again then, against my better judgment, nodded and waved him toward the chair. He smiled slightly and turned to sit. I followed him, but paused to pick up my scotch from behind the picture.

To hell with propriety, I really needed that drink just then.

"Make it fast," I said after taking a sip. "I've got an appointment in half an hour, and..."

My butt hit the chair and I lost my train of thought in shock. The glass tumbled from my hand and fell to the floor, somehow not shattering as it struck the hardwood floor with a dull thud. I did not have hardwood floors in my office.

My chair, a comfortable leather unit, was not the chair I landed in. I could feel hard slats on my back and the arms were thin, made of wood. Looking down, the rest of the chair was wooden as well. The seat was covered in a quilted cushion and I knew without looking that the legs ended on long wooden rockers.

Directly in front of me, the fire crackled and popped in the fireplace as it always did, and the narrow door stood closed off to the right.

Almost dreading to do it, I turned my head to the left, slowly. And saw Bartleby sitting in his rocking chair next to me, a twinkle in his eye and a wry smile on his lips.

"I thought a more familiar setting might make the conversation go more smoothly," he said. Gesturing toward the table between us, he added, "I'm afraid I don't have any scotch, but would you like some hot chocolate?"

Dazed, I nodded slowly. My hand trembled as I took the steaming cup closest to me on the table. My rational mind shouted out in denial of what was happening, but the rich flavor of the chocolate touching my tongue overpowered that thought. It could not be, but at the same time I could not deny that it was real.

"What is this place?" I said as I lowered the mug from my lips. I was amazed that I did not stammer.

"Between worlds," Bartleby said before taking a sip himself. "Here I meet with champions and potentials in safety and privacy, so the enemy does not know of them before they are ready for the burden."

Champions? Potentials? What was he talking about?

He must have seen the confusion on my face because he sniffed softly and spoke again. "Shakespeare was more correct than he knew. There are more things in heaven and earth than you ever dreamt of, young knight. But in the end all things serve either the Light or the Dark. The balance between the two is what keeps the universe in motion and makes life possible. But from time to time the Dark will rise up and attempt to disrupt that balance. When that happens, the Light selects a champion whose task it is to restore the universe to the way it should be." He tapped his index finger on the storybook he still held on his lap.

"The knight," I said, and he nodded. "So those storybooks are..."

"The records of the exploits of previous champions, yes." Bartleby smiled again and nodded in approval. "You are quick. Quicker than many of your brothers."

I felt my eyebrows quirking upward and shook my head. "I don't have any brothers or sisters."

"Ah but you do, young knight. Not physical siblings, to be sure. But spiritual ones." Again he tapped the storybook. I got a sinking feeling in the pit of my stomach.

"What do you mean?"

Bartleby turned his head away and focused on the flames. He sat in silence long enough that I almost stood up to wave a hand in front of his face. He chuckled softly. "That will not be necessary, young knight. I am quite well."

His words were like being punched in the gut. I felt my eyes bulging and realized I was clenching my hands on the arms of the rocking chair.

Bartleby, seemingly oblivious to the affect his words had on me, continued. "Every generation is a continuation of the struggle between Light and Dark, young knight, and can remake the universe as it sees fit. Because of that, both sides watch the incoming generations with interest and seek out potential champions."

"Through their dreams."

Bartleby nodded again. "Think of it as a spiritual radio wave. Those who have the ability to hear and who are inclined toward the Light join me here for instruction and guidance, so when the time comes they may make their choice knowledgeably."

"So you work for God. What are you, some kind of angel?"

Bartleby snorted slightly and smirked. "That is a gross simplification. But if it helps you to think in such terms, then yes. I work for God."

I groaned and leaned back in my rocking chair. This was all coming a bit too quickly. I took a deep gulp of hot chocolate and swallowed. Warmth flowed into me from the liquid, but also a feeling of well-being. My stress lessened until it was almost gone completely. Peering into the mug, I murmured, "That's good stuff."

Bartleby chuckled softly, but did not say anything.

We sat in silence while I nursed the mug and my thoughts. I expected to wake up at any moment, and even pinched myself to hurry it up. No dice; I was definitely awake. Crap.

"I suppose you're going to tell me now that I'm destined

to be the brave knight from your storybooks, and that you have a mission for me."

Bartleby shook his head briskly. "There is no destiny, only choice. The last champion countered the Dark's gambit so effectively that I hoped it would be a generation or more before it tried again. That is why you haven't seen me in so long." He sighed and lowered his gaze. "I was mistaken. So I now offer the choice to take up the emblem of Light to the potentials in your generation."

What did he mean, potentials? I looked around the room again to be sure I was not imagining things. No, I was alone. Where were these others? "Umm, Mr. Bartleby..."

"Just Bartleby, please. Or Cornelius, if you prefer."

"Ok. There's no one else here," I said. "Where are the others?"

He sniffed again and stood. "They all refused."

"Wait, what?" I stammered. "They *all* refused? I'm the last one you approached?"

He nodded.

Great. I was the last kid picked for the ball team; it had been years since I experienced that bit of humiliation. I forgot how much it sucked. "How many others were there?" Maybe it was not as bad as I thought.

"Four hundred and fifty-eight."

Wow. Way to make a guy feel good about himself.

Without looking at me, Bartleby strode over to the door and stopped. "I once said you were not ready to pass through this door, but that you might someday. This is that day." He looked back over his shoulder at me. "Will you come?"

I looked from his face to the door. I had seen it many times before and it was always plain, painted cream with a simple chrome doorknob. Now, looking at it more closely, there were designs carved or painted into the door. Subtle designs, easy to miss: stars, planets, people, animals, flowing water. I blinked my eyes and the designs faded, only to reappear after a moment of staring at the door. It reminded me of those annoying dot paintings that supposedly contained images if you just looked at them long enough, or from the right angle. I once spent most of an afternoon at a picture store in my local mall trying to pick out the image of a sailboat from one of those paintings, without success. I had no trouble this time, though.

I was already a bit spooked, but looking at that door suddenly gave me the willies. I swallowed again. "What's in there?"

"The universe," Bartleby replied simply.

He reached into his pocket and withdrew a keychain holding a number of small silver keys. He inserted one into the locking mechanism in the doorknob. There was a loud click, louder than a lock that size should have made, and the door quivered slightly in its frame, almost as if it were made of canvas and a brisk breeze had just passed over it. Bartleby took hold of the doorknob and twisted. The door came unlatched and opened smoothly inward.

Starlight streamed in through the door, and more than starlight. Awed, I found myself standing and walking over to stand next to Bartleby, my mug forgotten on the table.

There was nothing but space beyond the doorframe. And when I say space, I mean *space*. Stars gleamed everywhere, billions, trillions of them. A reddish nebula glowed above us and to the left. Straight ahead, a bluish cluster of stars gleamed brighter than the others. Off to the right, I could see a yellow-orange sun with a system of six planets revolving around it. Not far past it, a larger greenish-white star mothered its own small system of planets. As I watched, it became obvious that the stars were a loosely bound binary pair and were revolving slowly around each other.

"My God," I breathed and took a half-step forward, wanting to see more.

Bartleby's hand on my shoulder stopped me. "Be careful, young knight. Do not wander too far. As you are now, without my protection you would quickly perish beyond this doorway."

I nodded, not needing to ask him how. "Then why are you...?"

"If you are to become the Light's Champion, you must first see and understand the nature of the struggle, otherwise you cannot do what needs to be done."

I nodded again. "So if I go with you out there," I gestured toward the starscape beyond the door, "I'm committed."

"Only to learning," Bartleby replied. "Once you have seen all that I must show you, you will be free to accept the burden or not."

Except that he already said there was no one else to do it. I could say no, but if the forces of darkness, or whatever, were really gearing up and there was no one to stop them, it would probably mean Armageddon or something. Some choice, that. I drew a deep breath and smoothed back my hair, which must have been standing on end as jittery as I felt. "Alright," I said. "Let's go."

From the corner of my eye I saw Bartleby smile. Then he took my hand and stepped forward, through the door.

❦ 3 ❦

I followed, and found myself floating in the void of space, unsupported by anything except Bartleby's hand yet somehow comfortably warm and able to breath. I got a queasy feeling in the pit of my stomach, like during the drop from the top of the big hill at the start of a roller coaster. I remembered hearing the continuous feeling of being in free fall sometimes made Astronauts spacesick, and understood why. Then I found myself smirking and chuckling as I envisioned the great Knight of Light, or whatever the right title was, upchucking all over his teacher. Bartleby would not appreciate that, I suspected.

We drifted away from the door and I glanced back over my shoulder. The doorframe also floated in the void, unattached to anything. It was a very incongruous sight and I wondered where the rest of the building that housed the room was located. Then the door swung shut, apparently of its own accord, and it vanished completely.

A surge of panic filled me, and I grasped at Bartleby's arm frantically, like a man desperately trying to avoid falling off a cliff. There was no way back!

"Be calm, young knight," Bartleby said, and patted my clutching hand with his. "No harm will come to you while you remain with me."

"But..." I realized I sounded as frantic as I felt and took a deep breath, trying to will my fear away. "The door's gone."

Bartleby chuckled and swept his free hand out in front of us. "There are always more doors, young knight."

I looked forward and saw he spoke the truth. As his hand moved, dozens of doors shimmered in and out of view all around us. Like the other, they all hung in space mounted to nothing, though I had no doubt they all led somewhere.

"Whoa," I observed. Never let it be said that I am not eloquent when I have to be.

Bartleby smiled in what I assumed was amusement and looked away toward the reddish nebula.

There was no feeling of acceleration, but we began moving very quickly. The nebula grew larger and larger in my vision, and as it did its color faded and grew more dim until it vanished entirely. I blinked in confusion and looked around, wondering if perhaps we had missed it. Only when I looked behind us did I see it again, shrinking quickly in our wake and regaining its color the farther we got away from it. We must have passed directly through it, but I could not understand why I had not noticed as we did.

That question dominated my thoughts for a time and I did not realize that we were continuing to speed up until I looked around to the left and right and saw no stars. Or rather, I saw many fewer stars. Where before there were literally billions in every direction, now there were only a few scattered here and there. What had happened? I looked up, down, left, right and it was the same, just a handful of lights in the blackness of space.

Wait, it was not completely black. Off to the right and

below me there was a hazy smudge of light, and another past it. Further in the distance, at the very edge of perception, other dim smudges were scattered around the sky. Now that I knew what to look for, I soon saw hundreds, if not thousands of them.

My confusion must have been showing. Or maybe he just heard my thoughts again. Regardless of why, Bartleby touched my shoulder with his free hand and said, "Look back, young knight."

I did, and was totally floored.

I had seen deep space photographs from the Hubble; who has not in this day and age? But it is one thing to see a picture of a galaxy from a telescope. It is another thing to see a galaxy with your own eyes. That is what lay behind us - our galaxy in all its glory.

My breath caught in my throat as I beheld it. The bulge in the galactic center, complete with a thin beam of light shooting up and down from its core. The bright bar of stars passing through the center and connecting the major spiral arms. The arms themselves, blue with the light of young stars except where dust clouds eclipsed the light. Globular clusters in their orbits above and below the galactic plane. It was beautiful beyond words; the Hubble pictures did not even come close to doing it justice.

Beside me, Bartleby said, "The universe in balance is a lovely thing."

I somehow found my voice. "It is."

"Light balances Dark. Stars are born, live, grow old, and die. Their light goes out, but in the explosions of their deaths, they seed the universe with the material to create new light, and new life, elsewhere. Black Holes, such as the one at the center of your galaxy," he pointed toward the bulging bar in the center of the galaxy as he spoke, "devour all matter they encounter and even light itself. Yet as they eat, they create some of the greatest lights in the observable universe." His gesture moved from the bulge to the lines of light shooting out of it. "Some of them can outshine whole galaxies by themselves. I believe you call them Quasars,"

I nodded slowly and recalled hearing about those things before in science class, during one of our introduction to astronomy lectures. But I had never thought about it the way Bartleby described, never stopped to consider the balance of forces that drove it all. Looking at it that way, it all made sense.

"It's amazing," I said.

Bartleby nodded. "And delicate. Even a small disruption in the balance can have a disastrous affect."

The galaxy began shrinking and it took me a second to realize we were moving again. We travelled faster than I could begin to conceive; part of my mind shrieked that we had to be traveling faster than the speed of light and that was impossible. But impossible or not, we were doing it, apparently. The galaxy receded into just a hazy smudge, then vanished altogether. On either side, we passed other galaxies, some larger than the Milky Way, some much smaller. All passed by in a heartbeat. We zoomed through a few too; the stars streaming past almost looked like the warp drive effect in Star Trek, but it only lasted a heartbeat before we passed through.

Finally, we slowed again as another hazy smudge grew into a collection of stars in front of us. But this was different. There was no structure like in the Milky Way. No blue of new star formation. Only the dull red glow of old stars nearing their end. The galaxy, if you could even call it that, was disjointed, devoid of dust clouds. It had a center of mass; I could see where the glowing galactic bulge should have been.

But in its center there was only a globe of blackness where no stars shined and, from what I could tell, no light passed through from beyond.

"What is this?"

❧   4   ☙

artleby frowned. When he spoke, it was in a hushed voice and a tone of near infinite sadness. "Here the Dark was victorious. This was once a thriving galaxy similar to your own. Flourishing with life and joy, glowing and singing in the night. But we were not able to counter the Dark's plans, and you see the result." He gestured toward the blackness at the center of the galaxy. "Now the Black Hole is virtually all that remains, except for a few stars that slowly burn out the last of their lives giving light and warmth to planets long dead."

I shivered with sudden terror as I looked at the destruction before me and understood its enormity. The weight of what was happening seemed to settle onto me and I gasped. "Are you saying if I...if the Champion...does not succeed, the Milky Way will become like," I gestured toward the ruined galaxy, "*that?*"

Bartleby gave a little start, then looked at me and shook his head. "Not all at once." He took a deep breath and turned us away from the grisly sight. "What happened here is the result of many generations of failure and neglect. No," he patted my shoulder in a comforting manner, "our battles are fought in much smaller arenas. The consequences of victory or defeat can seem small, even inconsequential. But they are real, and the cost of failure can be larger than we at first believe. In this place, though we tried to help, the Dark was victorious so often, and for so long, that the people gradually stopped fighting and surrendered, to their ultimate destruction."

I shuddered and forced down the urge to look back as we flew away. "I see."

Bartleby was silent for a few minutes as once again galaxies zoomed past us on all sides. Imperceptibly we began to slow until, as we neared a shining blue, barred spiral galaxy similar to the Milky Way, we came to a complete stop. Bartleby waved his hand through the space in front of us and a closed door shimmered into view. He withdrew his keychain from his pocket and inserted a key into the doorknob. Then he paused and looked back at me.

"I brought you here so you can see the ultimate result if the Dark is not balanced; so you can understand the choice you now have to make," he said. He waited for a moment for the words to sink in, then he turned the key in the lock, pushed the door open, and stepped inside.

I followed and found myself back in Bartleby's sitting room. The fire burned just as brightly and merrily as it had before. The mugs were still on the table, and still steaming. Even my scotch glass lay on its side on the floor in front of the fireplace. It was as though we never left.

Bartleby closed and locked the door behind me then walked over to his rocking chair and sat down. Feeling more than a little uncertain about what was coming next, I took a moment to pick up my scotch glass before I took my own seat. We rocked for a time, the slow creaking of our chairs creating a soothing harmony with the crackling and popping from the fireplace. Gradually, the angst I felt from seeing the ruined galaxy lessened, moving to the back of my mind but not fading completely. Somehow I knew it would never go away altogether.

I was the first to break the silence. "The others all saw what you just showed me?"

Bartleby shrugged. "About half of them refused to see me at all. Only a third of the remainder agreed to join me here. Of those, a majority convinced themselves they were hallucinating and refused to go onward." He sighed and rubbed at his temples with his fingertips. "It is my fault. I should never have left your generation alone for so long. I lost so many potentials..."

His words drifted off into silence. Suddenly I felt less bitter about being the last guy called up from the bench. If that many people had not even made it this far, well, I guessed that actually made me special, in a way. I managed a half-smile as I considered that.

Bartleby chuckled, his good humor returning in time with my thoughts. "Did you ever have any doubt, young knight?" His eyes had a knowing twinkle as he turned to regard me. I got another nervous lump in my throat and made a quick shake of my head.

Bartleby smiled faintly. "It is time."

"Time?"

"To decide. Time moves on, and the champion will be needed soon."

I swallowed, forcing down another bout of nerves. "What do I have to do?"

Bartleby returned his gaze to the fire and spoke softly. "It is always different. The Dark's machinations are never easy to spot. All I can tell you is that you will know it when you see it."

That was not very encouraging. "You've got to be kidding me. That's it? Talk about a nebulous job description!"

Bartleby shrugged his shoulders. "You will know the champion of Dark when you see him. From there, it will not be difficult to ascertain what he is planning." He sighed. "Believe me, young knight. Determining what is to be done is not the problem; doing it is."

"You do realize there are over six billion people in the world? The odds of me ever meeting..."

"You will meet," Bartleby interrupted. "You will be drawn to each other like moths to a flame. It is the nature of the conflict. There can be no victor if the champions never meet."

"Great," I growled. "I thought you were the coach here. Is that all the advice you have for me?"

"My task is to instruct and prepare the champion, not to guide his steps on the path." Bartleby inhaled deeply. "If I knew what was going to happen and where, I, or my counterpart for the Dark, could just intercede directly and shape things as I wish." He shivered as though that thought was profoundly disturbing to him. "I, and the others of my kind, are servants. Nothing more. The universe is for you and yours. Whatever becomes of it is for *you* to decide, not I."

Bartleby's words made sense when I considered them. I suppose it came down to the age-old question of why God allows evil in the world if He really is all powerful. I remembered asking that question myself. The answer given by a gruff old priest who happened to be sitting next to on the bus one day, Free Will, was not very satisfying. But looking at it again, in light of Bartleby's words, it made more sense.

I nodded slowly. "What happens if I say no?"

Bartleby leaned back in his chair and slowly exhaled. "Then there will be no champion of the Light in this generation, and the Dark will win by forfeit. It will fall to the next generation to resume the fight, when they are able to and assuming they are willing." He paused for a moment before adding, "But with each generation that goes by without a willing champion, the number of potentials will grow smaller until, eventually, there will be none left and the Dark will win completely."

"And then we become that galaxy you showed me."

"Eventually, yes."

I blew out a long breath. Talk about crappy choices. Another question occurred to me then. "Don't the Dark champions know what will happen in the end? Why do they do it?"

Bartleby quirked one eyebrow and snorted. "I doubt very much they are allowed to see the end results of their efforts, young knight. As to why, they do it for the same reason wicked men always do what they do: power, money, sex. Their hearts are greedy and they only see their own desires, not the affect their desires could have on others." He spread his hands in an almost helpless gesture.

I nodded again. There were always people who tried to get ahead by gaming the system or taking advantage of others. I heard stories about them every day in the news; why would people not behave the same way in the spiritual realm?

We were silent for a minute. Bartleby apparently had nothing else to say; I knew it was my time to speak. Yes or no. It was as simple as that. But at the same time, it was not simple at all. If I said yes, what was I getting myself into? Did Bartleby really intend me to go running around fighting Dark champions in the street like some sort of demented super-hero wannabe? I almost refused because of how ridiculous that would be, let alone how dangerous. But then again, he had said the arena of conflict was small, almost inconsequential. Looking at it in that light, the task did not seem like such a big deal at all. If only there was some way of knowing.

Then the image of the ruined galaxy came back into the forefront of my mind, and I realized it did not matter. Everyone else had said no. There was just me against...that. A small voice in my head whispered that would not happen just because I said no. Let the next group of guys handle it. I snarled at myself and forced the voice down. A real man does not shove responsibility onto someone else because he is afraid it might be too big. He bucks up, picks up his load, and does the best he can with it.

Or at least that was what I told myself as I stood up and turned to face Bartleby.

"Ok, I'll do it."

Bartleby nodded and stood as well. Stepping over to me, he reached out and placed his hands on my shoulders. "I am very glad to hear that." A broad smile crossed his face and his eyes seemed to shine in the firelight. Then he dipped his hand into his other pocket.

The object he withdrew flashed golden in the firelight. As he held it up before my face, I saw it was a flat golden disk hanging from a gold chain. The disk rotated around its clasp, and my breath caught in my throat. The front of the disk was inlaid in some sort of stone that caught the firelight and refracted it into a multitude of colors. The closest thing I could think to compare it to was an opal, but the shimmering colors in this stone put the best opals to shame. The stone was all of one piece and cut into the shape of a starburst. It was stunning.

Bartleby lifted the chain over my head, saying, "This is the emblem of the Light. You must never let it leave your possession. While you wear it, it will give you the ability to sense the Dark's powers and give you a measure of protection from them."

I bent my head and he draped the emblem around my neck. As the disk came to rest on my chest, I felt warmth and a sense of well-being and strength emanate from it into me. My skin tingled and I felt as though I could run a marathon at an Olympic pace. My mouth dropped open in awe, but I could not find any words to reply to Bartleby.

He apparently was used to this reaction as he smiled kindly and said, "You will become used to it." Then he raised his hands again and placed his palms on my temples. He closed his eyes and his lips moved as though he was chanting something, but no noise reached my ears.

A flash of light engulfed my vision and I felt myself falling limply from his grasp. Faintly, I heard him say, "Good luck, Sir Knight. May you be victorious."

Then it all went black.

❀   5   ❀

"Ace. Hey Ace!"

Jim's voice may have been enough to wake me up on its own given time, but he also shook my shoulders. Hard. I jerked awake and for a moment I could not figure out where I was. Comfortable padding beneath my backside and against my back. Bright lights. Pictures of various houses and buildings on the walls. And Jim's face hovering over mine, wearing an annoyed expression.

Then it hit me. My office.

"Were you out partying last night or something? Get up, he's going to be here soon!"

He? What was Jim talking about... Then it all came back to me. Giobald Capano, the firm's new client, had an appointment with me and Jim at eleven o'clock. What time was it? I found the clock on the wall and blinked. Ten fifty-seven. Crap.

"Sorry, Jim," I murmured as I pushed myself to my feet. My scotch glass was in my hand still. I had not slept well last night, nerves from the morning meeting and all. Between that and the scotch, I must have drifted off. That was one hell of a dream, though. I had not had a dream like that since I was a kid.

I put the scotch glass back into my bureau next to the bottle and turned back to Jim, exhaling deeply.

"You ready for this, Ace?"

I nodded. "Yeah, good to go. Let's..." As I turned, something moved beneath my shirt and I felt it thump into my chest. "What the hell," I said and reached up to my neck. And found a chain necklace there. My heart skipped a beat. It couldn't be.

But it was. I pulled the chain out of my shirt and looked at the stone-inlaid gold disk Bartleby gave me. "Holy shit," I breathed. It had really happened.

"Wow, nice," Jim said, leaning forward to look at the emblem of the Light more closely. "What is that, opal? Where did you get it?"

I cleared my throat and lowered the chain back into my shirt. "Ah, Jill," I lied. "She saw it on her trip to Sydney last week and thought I would like it."

Jim whistled softly. "That girl's a keeper, Ace." He grinned at me and then jerked his thumb toward my office door. "Let's get this show on the road."

I nodded and followed him out.

The firm's conference room was located down the hall and to the right from my office. It was a standard conference room: a long plain table with chairs to accommodate all comers and a teleconference microphone for each, a flat screen on one wall with a video camera mounted above it for showing presentations or conducting video teleconferences, a smaller table over to the side with a workstation to control the presentation, and broad windows displaying a great view of the harbor.

Jim and I were not the first to arrive. Linda and Jonas, my two direct reports, were busy putting the final touches on the room preparations: setting out glasses and pitchers of water and getting the firm's welcoming presentation up and ready on the workstation. As we walked in, Linda nodded at me and flashed a quick smile.

"All set," she said.

"That's good," I began, but stopped as voices in the hall drew my attention away.

A moment later, Lawrence O'Toole, the firm's owner and general manager, walked into the room, leading a short man in an obviously tailor-made suit. I recognized Giobald Capano from the picture in his client file, but he made a much stronger impression in person.

In his early 40s probably, he was bald, the kind of bald that spoke of frequent shaving with a straight razor more than natural hair loss, and slender, with a plain face that would go unnoticed in a crowd. He moved with an efficient ease that screamed of confidence and strength under control and he wore an easy, knowing smile on his face, as though he saw something funny that no one else in the room noticed.

I took all that in at a glance, but froze, my heart beginning to pound in my chest, as I noticed one other feature about him. His left ear was pierced by a silver earring that had what would probably pass for a black pearl embedded within it. But there was something not right about it. The pearl was more than black. It...oozed...darkness, seeming to suck in the light all around it, leaving the left side of Capano's face more shadowed than the right.

The room felt suddenly cold and I swallowed. I knew without having to ask. The Dark Champion. My new client was the Dark Champion. Son. Of. A. Bitch.

Lawrence made introductions and I remember shaking hands with Capano and saying some nicety or other. But my thoughts whirled and I was not sure what I said. How the hell was this going to work? Capano was wealthy, obviously, and had a lot of contacts in some very influential circles. Getting his account and keeping him satisfied was going to be a huge boon for the firm. Word was, he was here specifically because of my design reputation. It was flattering to hear that when Jim and Lawrence first told me of it last week. But now...

Now, Capano's desire to work with me seemed more sinister. Could he have known? No, of course not. It was a coincidence, nothing more. Like Bartleby said, we were drawn to each other. Probably had been for some time and without either of us knowing it. It made me wonder how many other people I had associated with over the years were potential champions.

That was a thought for another time. I needed to get it together and not screw up this meeting. Whether Capano and I were suppose to come to blows or not, it was not going to happen here and I certainly did not want to mess thing up with my bosses by screwing up this meeting.

So I sat down with the others and listened dutifully as Jim took over his part of the introduction presentation. Then, after a few minutes, it was my turn.

As I stood, my mind was still somewhat awhirl. Fortunately, this standard presentation was like second nature because I had given it so many times in the past. So I spoke from my script and did my part, then introduced Linda and Jonas, who presented their curricula vitae succinctly.

Then all eyes turned to Capano.

He was silent for a moment, his lips pursed in thought. Then he smiled again and leaned forward, tapping at the tabletop with his index finger. "I have heard good things about this firm," he said. Then he directed his gaze at me and his eyebrows lifted high on his forehead. "And I very much enjoyed what you did with Kevin McIntosh's house in Miami, Mr. Williams."

I blinked. McIntosh? His was one of the first houses I

helped design coming out of college, as a junior architect at a small firm in Miami. McIntosh was well off, but did not come close to matching the wealth of the people who frequented my current firm. I never actually met with him and I was not entirely sure if he would have heard my name at all since the team leader got all the design credit.

So...how did Capano know what I did on that job?

All that flashed through my head in a second. I simply smiled and nodded. "Thank you. That was a good job to break into the business from."

Capano smirked slightly and gave the briefest of nods. Then he clapped his hands and stood up abruptly. "Thank you, gentlemen. Ladies," he added with a nod toward Linda. "It will a pleasure doing business with you, I'm sure."

Lawrence and Jim exchanged glances at each other from across the table and slowly stood. I understood their confusion; usually these meetings lasted longer than this.

Lawrence cleared his throat and smiled professionally. "We are looking forward to it, Mr. Capano. I'll have Jim get in touch with your office to schedule a follow-up after his team has surveyed your current residence and completed some initial sketches ready for your review..."

Capano waved a dismissive hand at Lawrence. "Yes, yes. That will be quite satisfactory." He flashed a smile at Lawrence, then turned his eyes toward me. "Would you give me a moment alone with Mr. Williams, please?"

Eyebrows lifted all around the table. Jim and Lawrence both turned to stare at me in confusion for a moment. The question was written all over their faces: what's going on between you and our new client, Ace? But they knew better than to ask. Lawrence simply said, "Of course," and gestured for the others to leave the room. He followed them out, only pausing to shoot me a glance that promised a grilling later before pushing the door shut.

I swallowed and looked at Capano apprehensively, but did not say anything. It was his dime; let him talk first.

He just stood there, his hands resting on the back of his chair, and looked at me with a sardonic, knowing grin. It went on like that for several moments, then he chuckled softly and walked over toward me.

"Well, well," he said. "I must say I never expected it would end up being a guy like you." His tone was amused, mocking, to match the grin on his face.

"Is that right," I stated in as even a tone as I could manage. He knew me, just as I had known him on sight. That should not have surprised me, but it did.

Capano nodded and continued his slow, even pace around the table to my chair. "You needn't worry...Ace," he said, putting a little extra mockery into my nickname as he spoke it. "I won't pull the account from your firm over this. I see no reason we can't get along professionally." He reached the chair next to mine and bent over so that his head was level with me. He reached out and gave my shoulder a companionable squeeze that was perhaps just a little bit too strong. "Do not cross me, Ace. I am not a man to be trifled with." He smiled then, a broad smile that could almost be mistaken for one of friendship except for the naked malice in his eyes. "Are we clear?"

At his touch, a shiver of fear went up my spine. His grasp was cold and felt somehow unclean. It was also very strong; clearly he worked out a lot, which was more than I could claim. But I had interacted with pompous, fit guys who tried to be intimidating before. Capano, though...looking into his eyes I could tell he meant every word he was saying.

I pulled away from his grasp and said, "We're clear." I managed to impress myself by keeping my voice level.

Capano nodded once then turned and walked briskly from the room. I saw him nod to someone out in the hallway,

Lawrence or Jim no doubt, before the door swung shut behind him.

As the door shut, tension flooded out of me in a rush. I slumped forward and rested my head in my hands, exhaling forcefully. "Holy crap," I muttered to myself.

$\maltese$ 6 $\maltese$

This was going to get ugly.

But then, what did I expect when I agreed to do it? A walk in the park to the music of harps?

I shook my head and took a deep breath, then forced myself to my feet and smoothed my hair. This was not the time to lose it.

Lawrence and Jim were waiting in the hallway as I stepped out of the conference room, concern and curiosity etched on their faces.

"Ace," Jim said. "What was that? Is..."

I interrupted him with the quickest lie I could think of. "He just wanted to ask a question about the McIntosh house. How we could apply some of the designs into his. That's all. No problem."

Eyebrows quirked upward again and I could tell neither man was satisfied with my explanation, but I did not give them time to question me further.

"Excuse me, guys. I'm meeting Jill for lunch in twenty minutes," I said. Which was totally true, but also a cop-out.

But it worked; they did not accost me further as I walked away.

I took a minute to grab my car keys from my office and hurried out. The firm is on the tenth floor of a commercial high rise near the waterfront. I had a reserved parking spot in the garage beneath the building - a nice perk. As I drove into the late morning traffic, I asked myself where I thought I was going. I was supposed to meet Jill as Bernardo's, a nice little bistro on the outskirts of downtown, but the morning's events had left me without an appetite. Well, that was not entirely true. I was hungry all right, but for answers, not food.

I tapped the bluetooth control on my steering wheel and said, "Call Jill." Jill answered on the second ring.

"Hi handsome."

"Hey babe. I'm sorry but I'm not going to make lunch. Something's come up here." As I spoke, I turned a corner and headed in the direction of the public library. What I needed was there. Probably.

"Oh," Jill responded. "That's funny, I was about to call and cancel on you, too. Mario asked me to take over one of Dave's projects since he's in the hospital, and I'm swamped."

"What happened to Dave?"

"Appendicitis."

"That sucks. I'll see you tonight and we'll talk about it then. Try not to pull your hair out."

"Yeah right."

She hung up as I pulled into the library's mostly empty parking lot. It had been a while since I spent any time in a library. These days, I did my research online. But it would probably be a good idea to not allow this research to be traced back to my home internet access. The library seemed a good, anonymous place.

As I expected, they had a number of public internet access terminals in the back corner of the main reading area.

The fee to use them was minimal, not that I cared either way, and the signup procedure simplicity in itself. Within minutes, I was ensconced at a terminal.

Giobald Capano. His name brought up several pages of search results. I was surprised to find one of the first was a Wikipedia article. That seemed a bit excessively pompous. It was good for me, though. I quickly learned more than I ever wanted to know about the man.

He started out as a busboy in Palermo and gradually worked his way into some of the local artsy circles. Somehow he convinced people to lend him money to buy a small building, which he refurbished into upscale apartments. From there he acquired numerous other real estate holdings and branched out into venture capital. He invested in numerous startups and had become known as a savvy commodities trader as well. He hobnobbed with heads of state and celebrities of all kinds and was on the Boards of several big name charities. And as if that were not enough, he spoke Italian, English, German, Japanese, and Chinese, was a blackbelt in Aikido, played the violin, and was dating a supermodel.

Not too intimidating. Not at all.

On paper, at least, he seemed like a standup guy, a pillar of the community, and all that good stuff. There had to be more. He was not the Dark champion because of his good deeds.

I finally found it on the fifth page of search results. A story on a small news blog in Georgia. Two years ago, a local man had been hiking in the hills and stumbled upon a ramshackle old cabin in a sheltered valley. It was falling apart, but inside the man found an intact lockbox that held a number of old documents. He went on to sell it to a collector: Giobald Capano. There was a picture of the two of them shaking hands in front of a local bank, where they had apparently sealed the deal.

It was nothing, really. A tiny story about a very minor event.

Besides historians, who cares, really, about a bunch of old papers? Yet the story leapt out at me. Even after I paged back to the search engine results list, that link among all the other seemed to pulsate, to glow more than the rest of the monitor's LCD display. There was no rational way to know it, but I did - this was it. Something about this little deal - well really not so little - Capano had paid the man five million dollars - was central to what has happening with Capano and me.

I printed out that article and went back to the office, stopping briefly for a Hardees hamburger.

I somehow managed to fend off the worst of Jim and Lawrence's questions with explanations that seemed lame to me but that apparently satisfied them. The rest of the afternoon, I tried in vain to get started on the design for Capano's house. I tasked Linda and Jonas with some of the basic designs and then sat at my desk trying to work on the overall plan. But the knowledge of who he was, the puzzle of the Georgia document purchase, and general angst over the entire situation left me unable to concentrate. I kept going over it all in my mind, but got nowhere.

Finally I left for home, feeling frustrated and confused.

I lived about twenty minutes from work, in the tenth floor corner unit in a condo building on the outskirts of town. Not the swankiest place in town, but it had a nice view of the downtown skyline and the rent was affordable. I had lived there for four years, ever since I moved up from Miami, and did not see the point in moving just because I got promoted to team leader under Jim last year.

My building had an offset parking garage with assigned spots, but I did not mind the short walk to the tenants' entrance. A little fresh air helped clear my head after a long day. The ride up the elevator was quick, and before long I was home, sweet home.

I fixed myself a scotch and sat in a stuffed chair facing the window. There I let my thoughts wander. What was so special about that find in Georgia? And how could it possibly pertain to the battle Bartleby described? I could not wrap my head around it. It's not like we were talking about a weapon, or some monumental document that would undercut people's belief systems or reveal that the entire economy was a lie, sending it crashing to the ground, never to return. It was mundane.

But apparently it was not that mundane, otherwise Capano would not have paid five million for it.

Crap.

We were supposed to go by Capano's current residence tomorrow. His assistant was going to show us some of his favorite pieces of art, furniture, and what have you that he wanted to accentuate in his new house. That might sound strange, but I had seen wealthy clients ask for more ludicrous things than that. One guy in Miami wanted an entire bedroom built for his prize-winning Chihuahua. He spent almost six figures on that room alone. So I had learned not to be surprised by a client's request.

But Capano inviting us - inviting me - into his home surprised me. It was almost like he was flaunting himself, daring me to take a shot at him. But that was silly. Why do that after warning me off in the conference room?

Jill arrived just then, breaking my chain of thought with, "Hey handsome," spoken in her melodious alto.

I stood up to greet her and we set about cooking dinner. Jill had a place across town, a nice little townhouse, but these days she spent more time here than there. I had not thought about it too much, or rather I had avoided thinking about it, but we were getting to the point where we would have to talk about the next step soon.

But not tonight. Tonight was for grilled filets, garlic mashed potatoes, and greens.

We spent a pleasant evening together. But I continued to be distracted by my new task and found myself making mono-syllabic answers to Jill's remarks from time to time. She noticed, and asked what was wrong. I managed to satisfy her with an explanation about a stressful day at work, which was true. But I could tell she wanted to know more. Maybe later, when I figured out how to tell her without making her call for the men in white coats with straightjackets.

Jill begged off spending the night; she had an early morning at work tomorrow. We said goodnight at around ten-thirty and I hit the sack.

And was unable to get to sleep. I tossed and turned for what felt like forever, my mind awhirl still. What was I going to do? What was I supposed to do?

Fatigue will win out over mental distress, though. I eventually drifted off, and was not at all surprised to find myself in Bartleby's sitting room again. As before, the old man was rocking in his chair, making soft creaking noises. Two steaming mugs sat on the table again as well.

I wasted no time, but walked over and stood in front of Bartleby with my hands on my hips. "Ok, Bartleby, you want to tell me what the hell I'm supposed to do here?"

7

One eyebrow twitched upward on the old man's brow and he gestured toward my rocking chair. "Why don't you tell me about it," he replied, his voice kind and patient.

With a sigh, I sat down and grabbed up my mug. In between sips of hot chocolate, I related my encounter with Capano in the conference room and what I had learned about him from my research. As I reached the end of my tale, Bartleby blew out a long breath, billowing the whiskers of his mustache slightly.

"Well," he said, "I can't say I've heard of the two champions meeting so quickly before." He rubbed at his nose with his index finger for a moment, then mused, "It's almost as though he was looking for you specifically."

"I thought that same thing," I replied. "But that's not possible, is it?"

Bartleby cleared his throat. "Normally, no. But your generation, as I stated before, is different. My presence masks the potentials from the Dark's notice. In your case..." He sighed and hung his head. "In your case, I thought there would not be need for your generation, so I left you alone.

Apparently in my absence, the Dark guide learned of your and the other potentials' identities. As they declined the task, one by one, it was probably just process of elimination to reach you."

"Well that's great," I spat. "So he's probably ready for me, whatever I do."

"That is possible."

I growled and took a longer drink from my mug.

"Now as to the object in question," Bartleby said, as though his last revelation was no big deal at all. "You must understand that our conflicts are not normally large."

"You said that before."

Bartleby nodded. "It may be that this object has a special significance for a few people, or maybe just one. Its presence, or lack, may be all that prevents or causes those people from going over to the Dark."

"How?"

"I cannot say without knowing more about the object. And really it is immaterial. The important part is the impact on the people around it." He looked at me with narrowed, shrewd eyes and pointed his index finger at me. "Remember, sir knight, even a single person's actions can have ripple effects that resonate long after he is gone and can alter the world greatly, for good or ill."

"Great," I said. "So what am I supposed to..."

"When you see the object in question," Bartleby interrupted, "you will know what to do."

"That's not terribly helpful."

"It is the best I can do. Good luck, Timothy."

I would have retorted harshly, but the sitting room faded away in favor of a scene so bizarre it had to be another dream. I recall resisting for a heartbeat, but then the dream took me and I slept, oblivious to the fact that I was dreaming, until my alarm clock woke me at my usual time the next morning.

The morning routine went as normal. I got into the office at 8:30 and sat down at my drafting table. Linda and Jonas had left their initial drawings from the day before on my desk when they left, but I was too distracted yesterday to do a good job of reviewing them. I spent twenty minutes looking the drawings over then pushed them away. I thought of several ways to improve on the drawings off the top of my head, but it was a good start overall.

At 9:30, after my morning meeting with them, we found Jim in front of Lawrence's office. The two men were exchanging quiet words, stopping quickly when the three of us arrived. Jim glanced at us - at me - then looked back at Lawrence and nodded. The two exchanged a meaningful look and Lawrence went back into his office.

"Ready to go?" Jim asked as he turned back to face us, his normal cheerful grin on his face.

I nodded and Jim led us down the corridor to the elevator.

The firm kept a van down in the garage for these sorts of excursions. The four of us piled in after loading our notebooks and other equipment into the back, then Jim got behind the wheel and drove us away. It was a forty-five minute drive to Capano's house. Nestled in the hills west of town, it looked over the countryside from an unobstructed vantage point. The view was amazing.

"Why the hell is he moving?" Linda breathed as we got out of the car.

"He bought some beachfront property," I replied in annoyance. She should have known that; it was in the client information packet we had all received when we were tapped for his account. But this was not the time or place to poke her for not doing her homework.

Capano's house, his estate really, had a huge set of arched double doors, carved simply from dark, reddish wood with narrow panes of glass inlaid so those within could see callers.

They swung open as we approached and a tall man, dark of skin and hair, stepped out to greet us. He was well dressed in a simple but elegant black suit and carried himself with erect poise that exuded confidence and professionalism.

"Good morning," he said with a shallow inclination of his head to us, "I am Jasper, Mr. Capano's personal assistant. You are from the architecture firm, yes?"

Jim responded in the affirmative and introduced us. Jasper acknowledged each of us with cool politeness, but I could tell he really was not all that interested. We were a task on the checklist for the day, nothing more.

"Mr. Capano regrets that he cannot be here to liaise with you himself, but pressing business prompted him to leave the country last night. You know how it is." He sniffed softly and flicked his eyes over us in a way that said, 'You *don't* know how it is, you peons. And you know that I know it.' Then after a heartbeat's pause, he said, "If you will follow me?" and walked back into the building.

"Abrupt, isn't he?" Jonas observed, earning himself a sharp look from Jim.

We followed him inside and Jasper proceeded to show us around Capano's house. It was, of course, huge and sprawling. But I was not prepared for its elegant simplicity and the highly tasteful way he decorated. I am not sure why; perhaps I thought the Dark champion would go for torture devices and pitchforks, or maybe decor along the lines of Montana's house in Scarface, gaudy and in poor taste. A silly thing to think, but that's how it was.

The dwelling revealed a man that I could probably come to like. His book collection was extensive and eclectic, as was the art on his walls. His furniture was plain, unadorned, but of the highest quality. He was a sports fan; one room was set aside as a home theater, which was lined with pictures of various famous sports figures and team emblems, his favorites

I assumed. I spied a few of my personal sports heroes up there as well. The overall impression was that of a man who appreciated the best things in life, but did not care about flamboyance. Again, not what I expected.

It took a good hour and a half to complete the walkthrough. There were a number of items Capano would want just so in his new residence. Pieces of art that needed to have custom-created displays, an annoying feature of the kitchen that he wanted removed, things along those lines. None would be particularly taxing, but taken together they required a lot of work to get it right. Which is why our firm's fees were so high.

From a professional standpoint, it was a productive trip. But by the end of the walkthrough, I began to get frustrated. The house said a lot about Capano, but there was nothing that gave even a hint of what his Dark plans might be.

Then I saw it. A small picture frame in his sitting room, mounted near a panoramic window. Within the frame was a yellowing page, not much larger than a sheet of letter-sized paper. It seemed to glow with an inner radiance that drew me, an almost magnetic pull to walk over and look at it.

"What is this?" I asked.

Jasper had already turned to leave the room but stopped and turned back to me, annoyance on his face. I suppose I had disturbed his carefully designed schedule for the walkthrough or something. His lips pursed and he shrugged slightly. "Mr. Capano has a fondness for antiques."

Really. I had not noticed from the rest of his decor. I kept that thought to myself. "It looks like the map of a coastline somewhere."

Jasper nodded. "The oldest known map of the Carolina coast. Mr. Capano bought it a few years ago. Now, if there are no other questions here, you really must see..."

His words faded from my hearing as I focused in on the

map. It was old, yellowing, faded, fraying at the edges, and torn. One place in particular was distinctively marked as though it was important for some reason, but the writing there was so faded I could not make it out. If only...

"Ace, come on!" Jim tugged on my arm, breaking me from my contemplation.

I jumped, startled, and gave him a sheepish smile. "Sorry."

He looked askance at me and opened his mouth to speak again, but I stepped past him and out of the room, hurrying to catch up with Jasper and the other two in the hallway. It was an effort; I still felt the magnetic attraction to that map. I knew for certain that it was the document Capano had purchased from the man in Georgia. That meant it was important, somehow. I needed to find out why.

Back at the office, I set my team to work then went to my desk to ponder. Capano's demands for his house were exacting. But then, he was going to spend I did not want to think about how many millions of dollars for a brand new house at the beach, so why should he not get exactly what he wanted?

I blinked and leaned forward in my office chair, my eyes widening as it hit me.

A brand new beach house.

❧ 8 ❧

With a strangled cry, I turned to my bureau, pulled out Capano's client information packet, and leafed through it hurriedly. It was here. It had to be. And there it was - the address of Capano's new house, complete with overhead shots Jim or Lawrence probably obtained from Google Earth. But they were zoomed in too tight. I swallowed and turned to my computer then entered the address into Google Maps and waited for the page to update. It was zoomed in close, so I clicked out a few times.

I leaned back in my chair and stared at the screen for a moment. A chill went down my spine and I realized I was getting goosebumps, but not from the cold. The map showed the same coastline as the map on Capano's wall. And his property was in the exact spot that had been marked as important on that map. That could not be a coincidence.

What was I going to do? No sooner had I asked myself that question than the answer came to me. It was obvious; the only problem was getting Jim to agree to it.

It was easier than I thought it would be.

My flight departed at 7 am. I almost missed my connection in Charlotte because of weather in the mid-west, but it worked out and I landed in Hilton Head, South Carolina at 2 o'clock in the afternoon.

The humidity was the first thing to hit me as I walked out of the airport. It had been years since I last came below the Mason Dixon line; I immediately began to sweat. A little voice in the back of my head asked me why the hell I had come down to this furnace of a place, and why I had worn slacks and long sleeves instead of a t-shirt and shorts. But I did not waste time standing around. Instead, I strode over to my rental car and cranked up the air conditioning.

I checked into a small timeshare condo a few blocks back from the beach. I was not planning to stay long. Just long enough to survey Capano's new lot, take some pictures, and get a feel for the local utility arrangements so we would have a better starting point for the design. At least that was what I told Jim. He ate it up and wasted no time in having the firm fork over money for the trip.

I did not eat on the plane, so I took a few minutes to wolf down a quick lunch, then hit the road.

Capano's lot was not strictly speaking an ocean view. Situated at the southern tip of the island, it actually looked out into the Calibogue Sound between Hilton Head and Daufuskie Island. But there was a beach, his house would be right on it, and if he turned his head to the left he could see the actual ocean, so I supposed it was close enough.

I pulled to a stop a few houses down from his lot and got out of the car, camera in hand. The street was wooded, with expensive-looking houses, some more palaces than houses and several probably condo-ized from the look of them, everywhere I looked. Looking back and forth along the street, though, I frowned. There was something not right about this.

As I walked the few hundred feet from my car to

Capano's lot, I mulled over where that feeling came from. Then it hit me.

Capano preferred simple elegance. That was obvious from his manner of dress and his house in the hills. This place was...too cluttered, almost. The houses, big as they were, were too close together. The trees growing everywhere made it the outdoors seem enclosed. The whole block did not suit Capano at all.

And then I saw his new property. It was long and narrow, backing up to the beach. An older house stood about a third of the way back on the lot. It was not as large as its neighbors, though it was by no means small. Brown wood siding, a screened in porch in front, a detached two-car garage: it was definitely not to his taste.

Which is why we was tearing it down to build a new house, a voice in the back of my head said.

Maybe, but I was certain he bought this place was because of that map, not the lot itself.

I walked up the driveway, noticing recent survey markings along the lot's boundaries, and snapped off a few pictures. Jim would crucify me if I did not come back with something usable for the design. And truth be told, it was important to know the lay of the land if I wanted the new design to be the best it could be.

But I was not really there for architecture.

I walked past the house and into the back yard, then blinked in surprise. A front-end loader with a backhoe attachment and a little bulldozer were parked there. It was a little early to start razing the lot, wasn't it?

Then I saw the hole.

It was about fifteen feet across, twenty feet long, and five to ten feet deep. Capano had clearly used the construction equipment to dig it out. Why? I walked to the edge of the hole and peered down.

My breath caught. There in the center of the hole was a carved statue of a woman. She sat on a rock, nursing a baby she held in her arms. Around both the baby's and mother's heads were halos. I had seen that image many times before. But never had I seen a rendition that actually glowed. This one did.

"The Madonna and child."

The masculine voice surprised me, making me jump and turn around in a rush.

I should not have been surprised to see Capano emerging from the back door of his house, but I was. He wore loose-fitting khakis and a blue polo shirt, but he walked with a quiet dignity that made his outfit seem formal.

"I knew you would come," he said, stepping from the back porch to the yard. "It was inevitable."

"It was necessary if we want to make the new house fit with its surroundings," I replied, my tongue thick in my mouth. I managed not to stammer, despite the anxiety, slowly growing into outright fear, that I felt.

Capano snorted. "Let's not play each other for fools, Mr. Williams. We both know why you are here."

I took a step back, maintaining distance between us as he moved to the edge of the hole. "I guess that makes one of us," I said, gesturing toward the statue.

Capano's eyes flicked down to it and he smirked. "Probably one of the oldest European artifacts in this area," he said. "Made by the French Huguenots who settled Port Royall in 1562. Or maybe the Spanish explorers in 1526, though I doubt they would have taken the time to carve statues on their journey."

"I imagine it's worth a bit of money. Is that why you bought this place?"

Again Capano snorted. "It is, but not that much. I spent far more on this lot than I could ever hope to make selling that thing." He said thing in a strange tone, almost as though he found the statue distasteful. Maybe he was one of those guys who does not approve of breastfeeding, but I doubted it. It went deeper than that.

"I guess you really wanted a beach house then. Can't say I blame you. It's nice around here."

"It is. But my house in Cancún is better."

I frowned but did not reply. I took a moment to look back down at the statue. The soft glow it gave off was clearly visible, even in the direct sunlight. Also, it seemed to...tug...on me. In almost the same way the map on Capano's wall had. This statue was important.

"Why do you want the statue?"

Capano cocked his head to the side, like a bird, and looked at me in silence for a moment. Then he shrugged. "I really do not."

"Then why...?"

"Are you a man of faith, Mr. Williams?"

I shrugged. "Haven't really thought about it."

Capano's eyebrow twitched upwards. Surprise? His voice was level as always when he spoke. "Faith is a strange thing. The people who carved that," he gestured to the statue again, "had faith in what it stood for."

"Ok," I said slowly. Where was he going with this?

Capano smirked and shook his head slightly. "You do not understand. No matter." He sighed deeply and looked at me with flat eyes. "I warned you not to cross me, Ace." His right hand slipped behind his back and emerged holding a semi-automatic handgun. He pointed it at me. "I'm sorry it had to come to this."

Despite the summer heat, I suddenly felt cold. I backed up another step and raised my hands. "You're going to shoot me? Here in broad daylight?"

Capano shrugged. "Why not? That house is vacant," he

pointed with his free hand toward the house to his left, "Foreclosure proceedings, or so I hear. That one," he pointed to the right, "is a vacation rental, but no one's in there until next week. And the old lady across the street is hard of hearing." His smirk widened into a wicked grin. "Couldn't resist following my little trail of breadcrumbs, could you?" He raised his voice a bit. "Boys!"

From the shadows behind the garage came two burly men. One was black, the other asian, but there was essentially no difference between them. They had no necks, their biceps were almost as big around as my thighs, and they wore murderous scowls beneath dead eyes. Both wore dark slacks and collared white shirts that were open at the neck, and handguns in shoulder holsters. One of them carried a canvas sack, the other a length of rope.

❀   9   ❀

"Oh crap," I muttered, and turned to run.

And was stopped within a step by the report of Capano's gun being fired and a piece of turf kicking up just in front of me.

"Next one goes in your chest," Capano said. "Don't move." He chuckled viciously. "It'll hurt less."

The two guys grabbed me. I tried to struggle, but I almost never work out and I certainly never learned how to fight; I was like putty in their hands. Inside of a minute, they tied me hand and foot, pulled the canvas bag over my head, and pulled the drawstring tight. Then they picked me up by my shoulders and feet.

I began swinging back and forth, and I heard one of the men counting.

"One."

What the...?

"Two."

Oh crap.

"Three."

I opened my mouth to speak, but all the came out was a

short scream as they released me and I fell somewhere; into the hole I thought. I landed with a soft splat; the bottom was more mud than dirt. Gotta love the high water table in the coastal south.

The breath left my lungs and I spent a moment coughing and gasping. The bag over my head did not help matters at all. It made breathing very difficult and was already unbearably hot. This was bad. Very bad.

"Enjoy your stay," Capano said from above me. Then he muttered something more quietly to the two men.

A moment later, I heard a loud engine start up - probably one of the digging machines in the yard. Then rocks, pebbles, and loose dirt fell on me and I felt a surge of dread. They were filling in the hole, with me in it! Dread turned to terror as I contemplated being buried alive.

I rolled away from the area where the dirt came down, but only managed to roll about three quarters of a turn before my shoulder struck something solid. The statue. But why was it still here? I thought getting it was the whole point?

The sounds from the digger grew louder again and I heard and felt another scoop of dirt fall into the hole. There would be time enough to figure out what was going on later. Now I needed to get the hell out of there. Somehow.

I squirmed around, trying in vain to get to my feet. All I managed to do was slam my cheek into the corner of the statue's base. I saw stars and felt a stabbing pain, then wetness as I began to bleed. Son of a...

Thoughts of complaint vanished as I realized what had just happened. Another pile of dirt fell down as I pushed with my feet, slowly maneuvering my hands to the statue's corner. I traced the edge with my fingers and felt a surge of hope. It was rough, almost sharp. Praying silently that I would have enough time, I squirmed around until I had the rope binding my hands running along the edge, then I started rubbing it back and forth.

It took forever. Or at least it seemed that way. But when you're tied up, blind in a pit and a thug is continually raining dirt and rocks down on you, time can be a little hard to judge. The side of the pit I'd just rolled away from was beginning to fill; my legs and lower abdomen were now covered in dirt. The weight of the earth was substantial, but I could still move, for now.

I was just beginning to think that by the time I got the rope cut I'd be buried anyway when the rope snapped. I stopped in surprised disbelief. It had worked!

Another pile of dirt falling down was all the encouragement I needed to get moving. I yanked my hands free of the rope and pulled the bag off of my head. Daylight made me cringe and clench my eyes shut, but that discomfort was nothing compared with the sheer bliss of fresh, cool air.

It says something that the South Carolina summer heat was cooler than the inside of that bag. I was tempted to sit there and just enjoy breathing, but I heard the digger coming back. There was no time to waste. I hauled myself out from under the dirt and set to work on the rope binding my feet. It took a lot less time to get the knot untied than it had to cut through the rope. By the time the thug dumped the next load of dirt, I was free and clambering to my feet.

The hole was about a third full, the dumped dirt making a sort of ramp up to one side, where the thug had been dumping it, no doubt. The statue was at my feet, but there was nothing else close to hand. I pondered for a moment, then hefted it. It was about two feet tall, but not terribly heavy, maybe thirty pounds. Part of me wanted to leave it behind and just go, but I knew the statue was the key to this whole thing. Plus, it might make a nice cudgel to hit the thugs with.

I saw the little bulldozer backing up from the lip of the hole. Its scoop was raised, so there was a good chance the thug at the wheel could not see me. I scrambled up the ramp of dirt, having to claw and dig my way up. By the time I reached the top and peeked above the rim of the hole, the bulldozer was scooping up another load of dirt. The asian guy was at the wheel alone. I glanced back around quickly and could not see the other thug. I ducked back down beneath the lip of the rim as the thug turned the bulldozer back toward the hole.

I waited, the bulldozer's noise growing louder by the second. Then the scoop appeared, moving forward above the lip of the hole. It stopped moving and I surged upward, pulling myself out of the hole completely. The scoop tipped forward, dumping out its load dirt, as I reached my feet.

The thug's eyes widened in surprise. He took his hands from the wheel, his right dipping toward his gun.

I had only seconds to act. I bounded forward, raising the statue in both hands as I leapt up onto the step beside the bulldozer driver's seat. The thug's eyes grew even wider as I brought the statue down full force.

CRACK! The statue struck the thug in the left shoulder. He bellowed and went over to the right, still in his seat. I struck again. This time the statue struck his head. His body went limp and he fell from the driver's seat, landing on the turf beside the bulldozer with a dull thud.

I stood there, amazed that my gambit had worked and gasping for breath, for several moments before I remembered the second thug. I was a sitting duck if he was lurking around somewhere.

But he was nowhere to be seen when I turned around to look. I did not stop to question where he went, I just ran as fast as I could back to my car.

Back at my room, I stripped off my clothes and took a long, cold shower, then got dressed in a clean shirt and khakis and drank several glasses of water. Once I was feeling human again, I sat down at the table where I had placed the statue and examined it.

Maybe it was well crafted back when it was made, but now it did not look like much. It was weathered, eroded by dozens of decades exposed to the elements. All the same, it was beautiful in its simple depiction of a woman's love for her child. I sniffed softly. Of course, this was not supposed to be just any child, or just any woman. But there were countless renditions of Madonna and Child in the world. Why was this one so important?

I turned the statue around on the table. To my eye, it still gave off a soft glow. But as I looked more closely, I could see the glow was not uniform. One place near the center of the statue, just below where Mary cradled the baby Jesus, glowed more strongly than the rest. I leaned forward and gasped. There, barely visible against the rest of the stone, were subtle cracks, as though there was a panel in the statue.

I felt around the cracks, my intuition telling me that the real prize was there, within the panel. How Capano missed it, I had no idea, but there it was!

Several minutes later, my elation turned to dejection. I could find no way to open it. No latch, no button, no lever, nothing. Maybe Capano had seen the panel after all, and simply failed to get it open. In lieu of accessing the treasure within, he simply decided to bury it so no one could have it. That seemed a fitting course of action for the Dark champion.

Which did not tell me how *I* was going to open it. After several minutes of trying, I ran out of ideas, except a crowbar or hammer, but that would destroy the rest of the statue so I did not want to go there. Frustrated, I stood up from the table and turned toward the condo's kitchenette. I needed another drink.

But as I turned away, I felt a tugging on my chest, something sliding. I looked down and saw the outline of the Light emblem beneath my shirt. Instead of hanging straight down, it hung at an angle - pointing toward the statue.

I hurriedly pulled the emblem out and saw that it, too, was glowing. The starburst symbol unerringly faced the statue no matter which way I turned. I felt a surge of excitement and sat back down at the table. The emblem began pulling toward the statue more forcefully, so I took the necklace off and held it closer. The emblem swung into the statue in the center of the small panel. There was a bright flash of pure white light, dazzling but not stunning, and the panel fell open with an soft CLICK.

I blinked away purplish spots from my eyes and as I removed the panel's contents: a leather-bound book that was held closed by a thong. A symbol I did not recognize, a coat of arms probably, was stamped into the front of the book. As I removed the thong - it was stiff with age - and opened the book, the pages crackled softly. I winced, hoping nothing had been damaged, and slowed down. The pages were yellowing, brittle. Fading letters, written in tight cursive, filled each page.

I recognized enough words from my High School Spanish class to identify the language, but there was no way I was going to be able to translate it. What's more, this thing was several hundred years old. If it was not handled correctly, it could be damaged or destroyed. I needed help.

A quick Google search on my laptop showed me where to go. I gathered up my things and hurried out to the car. A couple hours later, I drove into downtown Charleston and, after weaving through charming tree-lined streets, pulled into a parking garage on Wentworth Street.

The College of Charleston Department of Hispanic Studies advertised itself on its website as the largest organization of its kind in the southeast. They could translate the book if anyone could. On my way into town, I called ahead and found the Department Chair had office hours this afternoon. Pretty lucky, but I was beginning to think luck had nothing to do with it.

As I walked into the Chair's office, I was struck, as I usually am in academic institutions, by the feeling of calm scholarship about the place. I could feel the accumulated knowledge of the place oozing from the very walls.

Professor Miriam Escobar was a greying woman in her mid-50s, wearing jeans and a short-sleeved flowery shirt with a narrow collar. I liked her on sight. She was just finishing up with some students when I knocked on her door. She looked up, an eyebrow quirking upward as she saw me and what I carried.

"You must be the one who called," she said with a wry grin.

Nodding, I waited for the students to leave before stepping into her office, closing the door behind me. After introductions, I placed the statue and book down on her desk and explained quickly where I found it, leaving out the bit about guns and almost getting buried alive. This did not seem the right forum for that sort of discussion.

The Professor's eyebrows lifted again as I finished my story, and she clucked at her teeth with her tongue. "You would be surprised how often this sort of thing happens, Mr. Williams. Well," she said, picking up the book, "let's have a look." She opened the cover and looked inside.

Her eyes widened.

Three weeks later, I watched an interview on Good Morning American on the TV set in my firm's conference room. Giobald Capano, looking the epitome of understated elegance in his simple but expensive clothing, sat in a stuffed chair between Professor Escobar and another academic type, and flashed a winning smile at the anchor's question.

"It goes without saying," he said, his tone pleasant, ingratiating. "When we found the statue on my property, I knew it was important, so I had my associate contact Professor Escobar immediately."

"Where did you find it?"

He shrugged. "I came upon it while digging a swimming pool." He flashed his smile again. "Just dumb luck."

The anchor shook her head, affecting astonishment, then turned to the academic man I did not recognize. "Professor Goldstein, why is this find so significant?"

"Well, quite simply, this completely changes our understanding of early European colonization. Here we have the journal of a Spanish priest who started an parish in South

Carolina twenty years before what we thought were the first Europeans to settle in that region."

"And he did it," interjected Professor Escobar, "in a totally different manner than others elsewhere. Rather than taking advantage of the natives or seeking to convert them, he seems to have actually cared about their culture. When the next Europeans arrived, he appears to have gone out of his way to defend the natives from them."

"And paid for it with his life." Professor Goldstein managed to sound grieved by this fact.

The anchor sighed, a convincing expression of sorrow on her face for a moment. Then she looked back at Capano and brightened again. "Now, Mr. Capano, you took things one step further didn't you?"

Capano nodded. "After the professors informed me how important the find was, we realized there were probably more artifacts from the priest's parish on my property." He smiled broadly and managed to look almost angelic. "So I decided to donate that property to the College of Charleston, in the interest of science."

The anchor smiled along with Capano and shook her head. "Truly a generous gesture," she said as she turned to face the camera. "And a fitting cap to a story that sheds new light on a true man of compassion."

The segment ended, going to commercial, and I switched off the TV.

"Well," Jim said from the chair next to me, "it sucks we lost the Capano account, but I guess you can't fault his reasons."

"No, I guess not."

Jim stood up and clapped me on the shoulder. "Ah well, there's always next time." He strode to the conference room door and looked back at me with a grin. "It makes you feel good, though, doesn't it? To know that even back then there were people who stood up for those who could not defend themselves?"

I nodded. It did, and that was the point, wasn't it? That nice little story might influence someone else to goodness, or just brighten someone's day. It was small, but it was a victory, and who knows what its ultimate impact might be?

Jim left and I leaned back in my chair.

I thought long and hard, during the drive to Charleston, about how to play it, and decided going to the cops would have been useless; there were no witnesses to what happened, no evidence either way. It would be my word against Capano's, and I could easily see how that would turn out. Besides, was not the Light supposed to be the side of forgiveness and compassion?

I smiled, thinking about how it must have galled Capano to find out what happened, especially after the Professors contacted him. Yep, I'm a compassionate man.

MESSAGE FROM THE AUTHOR

Thank you for reading my book. I hope you enjoyed reading it as much as I enjoyed writing it.

Every review helps an author out, so whether you loved this book, hated it, or something in between, please take a minute to tell other readers what you thought. All of the online retailers make it very easy to do, and I would really appreciate it.

Feel free to come say hi at my website or on Facebook. I always enjoy hearing from readers, especially since you all are, collectively, my boss.

I also have a weekly podcast, Story Time With Michael Kingswood, where I read stories and talk through some of the latest goings on in my world. I'd love to see you there.

Thanks again. My best to you and yours.

Warm Regards,
Michael Kingswood

MAILING LIST

If you enjoyed this book and would like word on new releases and special deals from Michael Kingswood, sign up for his newsletter on his website. Guaranteed to be spam-free, you can opt out at any time. And you can rest assured he will not share your information with anyone, for any reason.

https://michaelkingswood.com/newsletter-signup/

SUPPORTING PATRONAGE

Michael would like to invite you to become a supporting member of his website. Similar in concept to Patreon, a few dollars a month will give you access to exclusive content, and help him to focus more of his time to writing fun and exciting stories for your enjoyment.

Sign up at his website:

https://www.michaelkingswood.com/membership/supporting-patronage/

ABOUT THE AUTHOR

Michael Kingswood is 20-year veteran of the US Navy submarine force and a lifelong fan of science fiction and fantasy literature. His work has appeared in numerous collections and anthologies, to include the Fiction River Anthology series from WMG publishing. He holds a bachelors degree in Mechanical Engineering as well as a Master of Engineering Management and a Master of Business Administration. He has four children and currently resides in San Diego.

Find Michael Kingswood online at:

www.michaelkingswood.com

www.facebook.com/michael.kingswood

steemit.com/@michaelkingswood

NOVELLAS

What Lurks Between

The Necromancer's Lair

The Champion

Veritas Morte

STORY COLLECTIONS

Tales Of Adventure #1

Tales Of Adventure #2

Short Story 10-Pack

A Jar Of Mixed Treats

SHORT FICTION

Michael has also published a number of shorter works, links to
which can be found on his website.

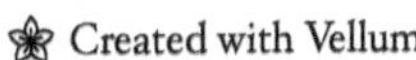 Created with Vellum